Music Magic

Written by
Jenny Moore

Illustrated by
Ellie O'Shea

Chapter 1

It was almost time for the Magic of Music Competition. The Willingford Witches had been practising hard all term.

Miss Minim tapped the music stand with her conductor's baton. "Good afternoon, girls," she said. "Are you ready for tomorrow's competition?"

"Yes," answered the witches.

Music Magic

Maverick

Chapter Readers

'Music Magic'
An original concept by Jenny Moore
© Jenny Moore 2022

Illustrated by Ellie O'Shea

Published by MAVERICK ARTS PUBLISHING LTD
Studio 11, City Business Centre, 6 Brighton Road,
Horsham, West Sussex, RH13 5BB
© Maverick Arts Publishing Limited August 2022
+44 (0)1403 256941

A CIP catalogue record for this book is available at the British Library.

ISBN 978-1-84886-908-0

www.maverickbooks.co.uk

This book is rated as: Lime Band (Guided Reading)

"Are you ready to wow those judges with your brilliant playing?" asked Miss Minim.

"Yes!" they said.

"Are you ready to win the Magic of Music Competition Cup?"

"YES!" they cheered.

Miss Minim beamed. "Excellent. I thought you might like to see this, before we start our final rehearsal." She held up a photo of a young witch receiving a gold cup from Albert Carper, the Minister for Magical Music. "This is me, when I was a pupil here," she said. "It was taken the year the Willingford Witches

Wind Band last won the Magic of Music Competition. It was one of the proudest moments of my life. But I'm going to be even prouder when I'm up on stage with you tomorrow. We're going to wow those judges *and* we're going to have fun. That's the most important part of all."

"But what about the Smugson School of Sorcery String Orchestra?" asked Lisa. "They *always* win." The Smugson Sorcerers and the Willingford Witches had been rivals for as long as anyone could remember.

"That's because they cheat and put everyone else off," said Rani.

"They won't put *us* off," said Miss Minim firmly. "We won't let them."

Chapter 2

Suki, the youngest witch, put up her hand. "I've never been in a music competition before. I'm feeling nervous," she admitted. "What if my clarinet starts squeaking?"

Miss Minim smiled. "Everyone gets a bit nervous before a competition. But there's nothing to worry about. A little squeak here and there won't matter."

"I'm nervous too," said Dalila.

"And me," said Yin. "I'm worried I'll split my bassoon reed."

"I know just the thing to get rid of nerves," said Miss Minim. "Put your instruments down, everyone. We're not going to *play* our first piece, we're going to *sing* it."

The witches giggled. That sounded like fun.

It *was* fun. Yin and the bassoon section put on their deepest voices for the low parts. Dalila and the flute section put on their highest, shrillest voices for the high tune. Suki even added in a few squeaks to make everyone laugh.

"That was brilliant," said Miss Minim. "And if you can *sing* your parts, you'll have no trouble *playing* them tomorrow. Let's try that one again from the beginning—with your instruments this time!"

"Wait, Miss Minim!" cried Lisa, putting up her hand again. "Something's happened to my music. The pages are all stuck together."

"So are mine," said Rani.

"And mine," said Yin.

Everyone's music was stuck.

"Look!" cried Dalila, pointing to a pair of boys in Smugson Sorcerer blazers disappearing out of the door. "They must have snuck into school while we were talking and put a sticking spell on our music. How will we manage now?"

Miss Minim frowned. "I'll make sure the pages are unstuck again in time for tomorrow," she said. "It's a tricky spell though, so we'll have to finish our rehearsal there. Don't worry," she added. "You're all so good, you don't need the practice anyway. And there won't be any magic cheating on the big day. The judges have tightened the rules this year: all magic wands are banned."

Chapter 3

The Willingford Witches were buzzing with excitement as their coach pulled into the music hall carpark. But their mood changed when they saw the Smugson Sorcerers' coach draw up beside them. The sorcerers pulled faces at the witches through the coach window and waved their wands as if they were practising spells.

"I thought magic wands were banned," said Dalila.

"They are," said Miss Minim. "Don't worry, they won't be allowed to take them into the hall." But she looked a little worried too, especially when the sorcerers' windows began to cloud up with glittery red smoke.

"Look!" said Yin. The sorcerers were leaving
their coach and heading towards the music hall,
still trailing faint plumes of smoke. "They don't
have their wands anymore."

"No," agreed Lisa. "But they *are* all carrying
spare bows. That's strange."

"And the conductor has got a spare baton," said Rani.

"Maybe they turned their wands into bows and batons to fool the judges," suggested Yin.

Dalila gasped. "What if they use them to cheat their way to victory?"

"Really girls, you mustn't worry about the Smugson Sorcerers," Miss Minim told them. But she looked more worried than ever.

Chapter 4

It was the Willingford Witches' turn to perform. They took their places on the stage and tuned their instruments.

"Ready?" asked Miss Minim.

Suki shook her head. "I don't think I can do this," she said, glancing at the Smugson Sorcerers. They were sitting in the front two rows of the audience, clutching their spare bows.

"What if something goes wrong? What if our music sheets get stuck together again?"

"Nothing's going to go wrong," said Miss Minim. "There's no magic allowed, remember." But even she seemed nervous.

"Forget about the audience," she told them. "Pretend they're not there. Or do what *I* do when I get nervous in competitions."

"What's that?" asked Rani.

Miss Minim winked. "I picture everyone in the audience with a sausage nose. And I do the same for the judges. I imagine their noses are sausages too."

The witches giggled.

"It works!" laughed Suki. "It really works. Thanks, Miss Minim."

"Excellent," said Miss Minim, with a grin.

"Let's show those sausage-nosed judges how good we are!"

Miss Minim's grin soon faded when the clarinet section started waving in panic, halfway through the first piece.

"Help!" mouthed Suki. "All the notes have vanished off our music. The sheets are completely blank! What shall we do?"

"Just try your best," whispered Miss Minim. "And if you can't remember the exact tune, then improvise. You can do it!"

The clarinets followed her advice, adding in impressive extra scales and fancy trills when they forgot the tune. They played better than they'd ever played before. And when Suki's clarinet let out a little squeak, she didn't let it stop her.

Miss Minim gave them a thumbs-up and grinned, as if to say 'Well done. Keep going.'

Chapter 5

The audience cheered when the witches finished their first piece. The Smugson Sorcerers weren't cheering though. They were scowling and whispering.

"Well done," said Miss Minim. "Let's see if we can make our second piece even better! Remember, whatever happens, *just keep playing.*"

The witches stared in shock at Miss Minim as she counted them in. Her conductor's baton had turned into a chocolate flake!

Miss Minim frowned as she kept time with her new baton. It was starting to melt under the hot stage lights. Her frown grew even deeper a few bars later, when the flutes' melody jumped up a whole octave.

"Help! Something strange has happened to our flutes," whispered Lisa. "Our notes are coming out too high."

Miss Minim's chocolate baton had completely melted now. She had to use her fingers to conduct instead. "Never mind," she said, with an encouraging smile. "Just keep playing."

But the flute notes kept getting higher and higher.

Soon they were too high for anyone to hear. The

local dogs could hear them though. There was a

loud barking sound from the back of the music

hall and two enormous dogs came charging down

the steps towards the stage.

"What's happening?" asked Rani. There were

three more dogs now.

"I think it's the flutes," said Dalila as a yappy poodle joined the fun. "Those super-high notes must sound like a dog whistle."

"Forget what I said," Miss Minim told the flute section. "*Don't* keep playing! Sing your part instead, just like in rehearsals yesterday."

It worked! The dogs stopped barking at once. They weren't racing round the hall anymore. They were listening to the music!

Chapter 6

It was time for the witches' last piece.

"I hope nothing goes wrong this time," said Yin, with a nervous glance at the Smugson Sorcerers. They were looking very pleased with themselves.

"Ready?" asked Miss Minim.

The witches nodded. But they weren't ready for the frogs that leapt out of the tubas after the first few bars of music.

Ribbit. Ribbit. Ribbit.

They weren't expecting the furry-faced hamster that emerged from Rani's saxophone, chasing after the frogs.

And *nobody* was prepared for the very last note, which came out like a big, wet raspberry.

The audience was laughing now, with the Smugson Sorcerers laughing hardest of all.

The witches waited for Miss Minim to tell them not to worry. They waited for her to say how brilliantly they'd played, despite everything. But Miss Minim was finally lost for words. She seemed too upset to say anything.

Chapter 7

The witches were in low spirits as they took their seats in the audience again.

"It's not fair," grumbled Lisa. "The Smugson Sorcerers cheated. They used magic to ruin our performance."

"We can't prove it though," said Dalila. "We didn't actually *see* them using their bows as magic wands."

Yin sighed. "I wish someone would use magic on them and see how *they* like it." But she was out of luck. There were no melting chocolate batons during the sorcerers' performance. There were no frogs leaping out of their cellos and double basses. They got through their pieces without a single problem.

"They're bound to win the cup again now," said Rani.

"I don't think I can bear to stay for the judging," said Miss Minim. The witches had never seen her look so frustrated. "Maybe I should wait outside."

"You can't let the Smugson Sorcerers see that you're upset," said Suki. "That's exactly what they want. If you leave now, then they've already won."

"Suki's right," said Yin. "We're the *real* winners anyway, because we've got you as our music teacher. You make everything such fun."

"Yes," agreed the other witches. "You're the best."

Miss Minim smiled. "Thank you, girls. I guess it takes more than dogs and frogs and rude-sounding notes to stop the Willingford Witches!"

Chapter 8

It took the judges a long time to make their decision. But the chief judge finally stood up and cleared his throat. "Ladies and gentlemen," he said. "It gives me great pleasure to announce the winners of this year's Magic of Music Competition. Congratulations to the..."

"WAIT!" came a loud cry from the audience.

Everyone turned to see an elderly wizard waving a camera in the air. It was Albert Carper, the Minister for Magical Music. The witches recognised him from Miss Minim's winners' photo. "The Smugson Sorcerers cheated," declared Albert.

"And I've got the evidence to prove it. I've just been rewatching the video footage and it clearly shows them casting a spell on the Willingford Witches, using their bows. That's why there were frogs jumping out of tubas. I *thought* it was strange.

It probably explains the dogs too." He tottered down to the judges' table to show them.

"Thank you, Minister," said the chief judge. "We did wonder where those frogs came from."

"It wasn't us," snarled the Smugsons' conductor. "That footage must have been faked."

"I hope you're not accusing the *Minister* of faking it?" said the judge, looking shocked. "I think I know how we can settle this matter once and for all though. As you know, contestants aren't allowed to use magic inside the hall. But there's nothing in the rules about *judges* using magic. A simple revealing spell should sort this out."

He pulled a wand from his judging robes and waved it at the Smugson Sorcerers. Everyone gasped as their bows turned back into magic wands.

"As we suspected," said the judge, frowning. "In that case, I've no choice but to disqualify the Smugson Sorcerers from the competition. But that doesn't change the result. This year's winners are... the Willingford Witches' Wind Band!

Congratulations on a brilliantly fun and original performance under tricky conditions. You've all shown real talent and determination today. Well done!"

Everyone cheered as Miss Minim and the witches trooped back onto the stage to claim the Magic of Music cup. Everyone *except* the Smugson Sorcerers.

"This calls for another winners' photo," said Miss Minim, as Albert presented them with the cup. "Say cheese everyone!"

"Cheese," chanted the witches, grinning with pride.

Discussion Points

1. What did Miss Minim's photo show?

2. Who were the Willingford Witches' rivals?

a) The Wicked Wizards

b) The Smugson Sorcerers

c) The Mean Magicians

3. What was your favourite part of the story?

4. Which instrument did Suki play?

5. Why do you think Miss Minim was upset?

6. Who was your favourite character and why?

7. There were moments in the story when **things didn't go to plan**. Where do you think the story shows this most?

8. What do you think happens after the end of the story?

Book Bands for Guided Reading

The Institute of Education book banding system is a scale of colours that reflects the various levels of reading difficulty. The bands are assigned by taking into account the content, the language style, the layout and phonics. Word, phrase and sentence level work is also taken into consideration.

The Maverick Readers Scheme is a bright, attractive range of books covering the pink to grey bands. All of these books have been book banded for guided reading to the industry standard and edited by a leading educational consultant.

To view the whole Maverick Readers scheme, visit our website at www.maverickearlyreaders.com

Or scan the QR code to view our scheme instantly!

Maverick Chapter Readers
(From Lime to Grey Band)